THE LEGEND OF THE
CHRISTMAS WITCH

DAN MURPHY & AUBREY PLAZA
illustrated by JULIA IREDALE

VIKING

VIKING

An imprint of Penguin Random House LLC, New York

First published in the United States of America by Viking,
an imprint of Penguin Random House LLC, 2021

Copyright © 2021 by Aubrey Plaza and Daniel Murphy

Visit us online at penguinrandomhouse.com.

Library of Congress Cataloging-in-Publication Data is available.

Manufactured in China

ISBN 9780593350805

10 9 8 7 6 5 4 3 2 1

RRD
Book design by Jim Hoover and Julia Iredale
Typeset in Fairy Tale, Decour Black, Sequel, and Australis Pro
The illustrations in this book were created with gouache and digital mediums.

For my parents, Elaine and Steve,
who taught me to love reading and storytelling. —D. M.

For my mom, a brave witch indeed. —A. P.

For Kymera and Ronan and all the little
ones who keep the Yule Fairies alive. —J. I.

PROLOGUE

'Twas the season of Yuletide,

And as the Cold Moon shone down,

The Christmas Witch traveled to each little town.

While Mother and Father slept soundly in bed

Some children snuck to their windows instead.

They fixed their eyes on the falling snow,

In hopes for a glimpse of the witch's shadow.

Like a wondrous phantom who smelled of the sea,

She whistled in the darkness a strange melody.

A wreath made of feathers, a doll made of hair,

Peculiar gifts left on the doorstep with care.

Tho' gathered at the window, they caught not a sight

As the Christmas Witch disappeared into the night . . .

No doubt you've never heard

the name of Kristtörn, for the Legend of the Christmas Witch is a story that has been forgotten to time. But in her day, she was as familiar to children as Santa Claus. In fact, she is his long-lost twin sister, who for many fated reasons ended up at the South Pole.

Stories and songs were written about her, yes. But as the years went on, these tales, told in whispers around the fire, became nothing more than scary stories meant to frighten children. Convinced of her evil nature, the elders were determined to erase all memory of her. And they have succeeded . . . until now.

The tale I'm about to tell may seem too fantastic to be true. But I assure you, it did happen. This is the real story of how Kristtörn became the Christmas Witch. And I should know—I was there.

—*M*

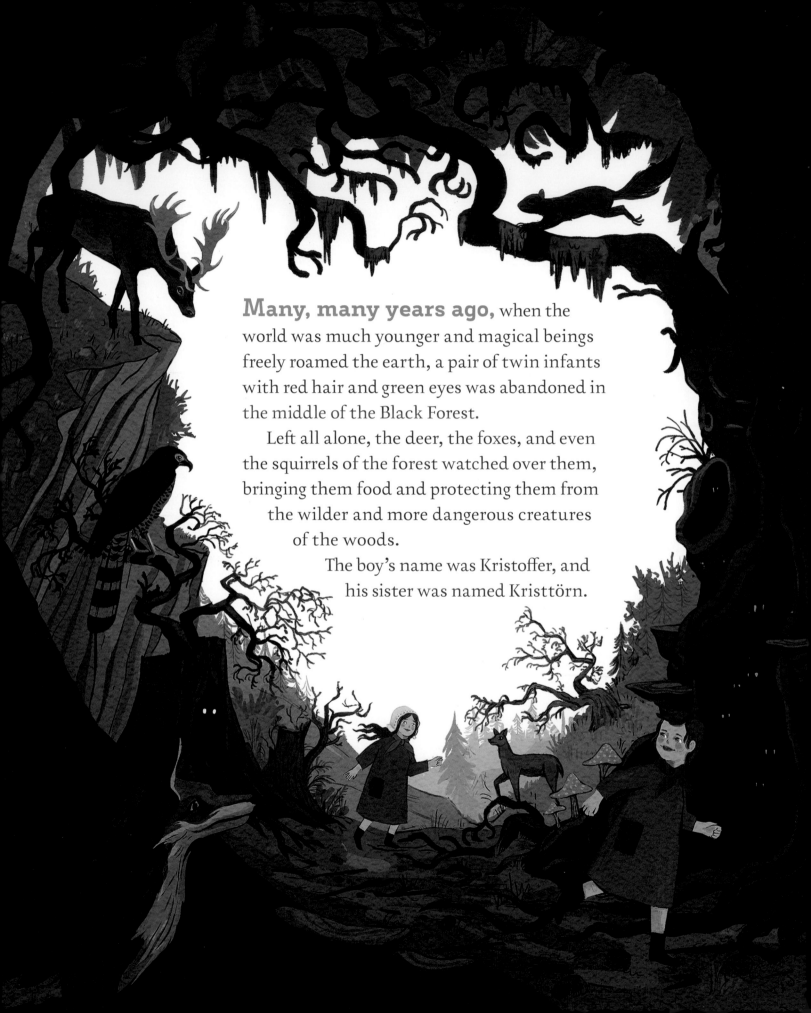

Many, many years ago, when the world was much younger and magical beings freely roamed the earth, a pair of twin infants with red hair and green eyes was abandoned in the middle of the Black Forest.

Left all alone, the deer, the foxes, and even the squirrels of the forest watched over them, bringing them food and protecting them from the wilder and more dangerous creatures of the woods.

The boy's name was Kristoffer, and his sister was named Kristtörn.

They were no ordinary pair of twins, for before long
they discovered they each had a unique set of gifts.
Kristtörn had the ability to talk to animals. And with
a touch of her hand, she was able to make trees and bushes
grow and produce fruit. The two of them never went hungry.

Kristoffer was able to disappear and reappear at will, and
both twins shared the gift of swiftness, running around the
woods at fantastic speeds. Their favorite game to play was
hide-and-seek, and each could hide from the other for many
hours before being found. Sometimes Kristtörn would leave a
trail of little gifts made of twigs and leaves from the forest for
Kristoffer to find.

As time passed, they developed their own secret way
of communicating by whistling, imitating the strange
melodies of their friend the nightingale.

At night, they would lie in the clearing and
count the stars in the heavens. Their bond was
deep and eternal.

It so happened that one day, while they were playing together, they heard two people talking nearby in the woods. They had never encountered other people, so Kristoffer whistled to his sister to go hide in a thicket, for he was as brave as she was shy.

By and by, a Danish couple by the name of Kringle came passing through the forest clearing heading north. It was then that the boy smelled the most delicious aroma he had ever smelled, and hesitantly approached them.

"Look at this young child!" they exclaimed, for they had always dreamed of having a family, but weren't able to have children of their own. "I wonder what his name is."

"My name is Kristoffer," he said. To his surprise, he was able to speak to them in their own language.

"Where are your parents, and why have they left you all alone?"

"I have no parents," he said, reaching toward the basket the woman was carrying, from which came that most enticing smell. She picked up the young boy in her arms and handed him a warm cinnamon roll from her basket.

Watching from the thicket, Kristtörn saw the woman pick up her brother. She called after them, fearing he was being kidnapped, but her cries only sounded like the mournful song of a nightingale. "Oh, what a beautiful bird!" the man exclaimed. "We will always remember how magical this forest was where we found this lad."

Kristoffer, delighted by the pastry, greedily reached for another and momentarily forgot about his sister as the new family journeyed on. Soon they could no longer hear her frantic song.

Now, without her brother, Kristtörn found herself truly alone, and she began to sob big angry tears. For three days and nights, she wept and wept, and no animal large or small could comfort her.

On the fourth day, a witch named Lutzelfrau heard her cries while gathering gray mushrooms with her raven friend perched on her shoulder. The old witch found Kristtörn in the thicket and noticed that a beautiful holly bush had sprung up in a perfect circle around the child, protecting her with sharp leaves that repelled the wild wolves hunting for food at dusk.

"Why do you cry, my child?" the witch asked, but this only made Kristtörn's tears flow faster. The old woman knelt down and stuck her bony hands into the bush to try to pick her up. But though she was careful, she pricked her little finger on the leaves and it began to bleed.

"Ouch!" Lutzelfrau shrieked. But then the child inside the bush reached out her own little finger and locked it with the witch's, and the wound immediately healed. Lutzelfrau was astonished to see that there remained not a scratch on her hand.

"This child is one with nature, and was born with a magic that may rival my own. She must be protected," she said to an old raven named Malachi, who flew close behind and caw-cawed in agreement.

With that, she pulled Kristtörn out of the bush, placed her in the large satchel around her neck, and took her back to her cottage. From that day on, Kristtörn was raised under Lutzelfrau's care.

The Kringles returned to Ålborg, and as they had no children of their own, decided to adopt Kristoffer. The husband, Johan, was an expert woodcutter and craftsman. The wife, Clara, a marvelous baker, was known in her village for a delicious pastry that she made each Christmas called kringle.

As Kristoffer grew up in the small port village along the Limfjord, his family instilled in him a strong sense of duty and hard work. He spent the days learning his father's trade, and was particularly fond of creating new toys that he would share with his friends in the village.

In the evenings, he would watch his mother bake breads and other sweets, and helped her to deliver them to the townsfolk on the family's sled.

Meanwhile, Kristtörn was living a wild, carefree life in the forest.
She cultivated her magical abilities under Lutzelfrau's watchful eye, and
found that she was a quick learner. At the same time, she could also lose
her temper quite easily when a spell wouldn't turn out quite right.

One time, out of frustration for a spell gone wrong, she kicked the side of a large old oak tree, making a huge dent in its side. But she was immediately sorry for what she had done.

"I vow to never lose my temper like that again," she said.

Sometimes at night, after the old woman was asleep,
Kristtörn would gaze out the window in the thatched roof
above her bed and count the stars. Somewhere, she felt sure,
in some other part of the world, her brother was doing the
same. And someday, she knew, she would follow the course
of those stars and find him.

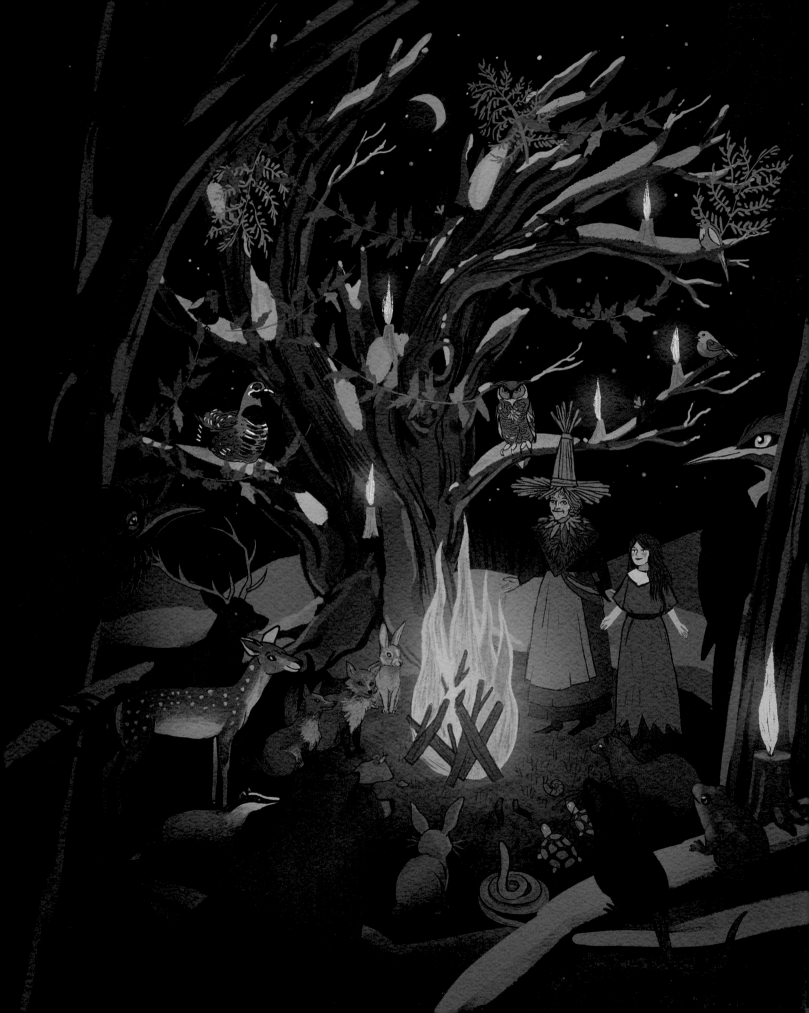

It was finally Yuletide, a celebration of the winter solstice, and Mother Lutzelfrau was known as the Yule Witch. This time of year the days were short and frozen, and the nights seemed as if they'd stretch on forever. Kristtörn would help her mother prepare for these celebrations. All the creatures of the forest would gather nightly around an enormous bonfire and hang evergreen and holly sprigs from the tree branches, singing ancient songs to the Cold Moon.

> *"Gather we under the Cold Moon's light,*
> *To come together this Yuletide Night!*
> *Birds of sky and beasts of land,*
> *'Round the fire, joining hands,*
> *Merrily celebrate the feast of old*
> *As we prepare for the winter's cold."*

Kristtörn came to have a deep love and appreciation for the Yuletide, and winter was always her favorite season.

Now, remember, readers, at this time in history, fears of witchcraft became widespread throughout the continent. Many villages chased their local witches out of the surrounding forests, rounding them up and burning them at the stake. Lutzelfrau often reminded Kristtörn, "You must always be careful, when you use your magic, to never been seen. You are unique, but not everyone will understand your power, and many will be fearful of it." But Kristtörn had led such a sheltered life that she hardly paid any heed to her mother's warning.

One day, as Kristtörn was picking berries, she came upon a small rabbit who had been struck by an arrow and was in a great deal of pain. She knelt down and cradled it in her arms.

A few moments later, a young hunter, a lanky boy with curly blond hair, came searching for his arrow and the rabbit he had shot. When he came upon Kristtörn, he watched with admiration as the young girl so gently tended to it.

"Could I have that rabbit, miss? I am going to make a stew for supper this evening!"

Kristtörn turned to him, flames of anger dancing in her eyes. "How could you harm this tiny creature?" she demanded. "What kind of wickedness consumes you?" She pulled the arrow out and pointed it at him menacingly.

Then he watched with horror as she healed the rabbit's wound with her other hand and it hopped back into the woods.

"Witchcraft!" he cried as he raced back to his village as quickly as he could. "There's a witch in the woods!"

Not two hours later, Malachi—Lutzelfrau's trusty messenger raven—came to her cottage with news that a mob was forming in the nearby village to find Kristtörn. Lutzelfrau had been waiting for this day, and knew deep in her heart that she needed to send the child away to save her life.

"I bring some news for Kristtörn, too," the raven said. "A friend of mine has just returned from the northern Scandinavian mountains and has seen her brother, Kristoffer, there. He lives very simply among the little elves called the nisser and raises a herd of reindeer."

Later that evening, as they sipped dandelion tea after supper, she broke the news of the mob to Kristtörn. "It's no longer safe for you to be here. It's time for you to travel far, far away to another part of the world."

Kristtörn begged her to let her stay. The old witch was unrelenting, but she did share Malachi's news of her brother.

"You have a destiny, my child," she said, poking at the leaves at the bottom of the girl's mug with her bony finger. "I cannot see exactly what it is yet, but it will take you to a distant shore, at the very tip of the earth."

"In that case, I will go north and find my brother," the girl said, comforted by the thought. "We were separated against our will in the forest, and I feel certain he is looking for me, too. He will protect me."

The next morning, they went down by the Rhine River and, using their magic, built a small boat out of pine wood. The old witch lined the boat with soft sheep's wool, and packed it with nuts and seeds that she had been storing away for the winter months. Into the bow of the boat, she tucked a holly tree sapling to remind Kristtörn of her home.

Then Lutzelfrau took her own cape, woven out of leaves and grasses from the forest floor, and placed it around Kristtörn's shoulders to keep her warm and dry.

"After I find Kristoffer, I will someday return for you, Mother," Kristtörn told her.

"How kind you are, Kristtörn, but I am old now and not much longer for this world. We may not see each other again, but Malachi here is never far and will watch out for you."

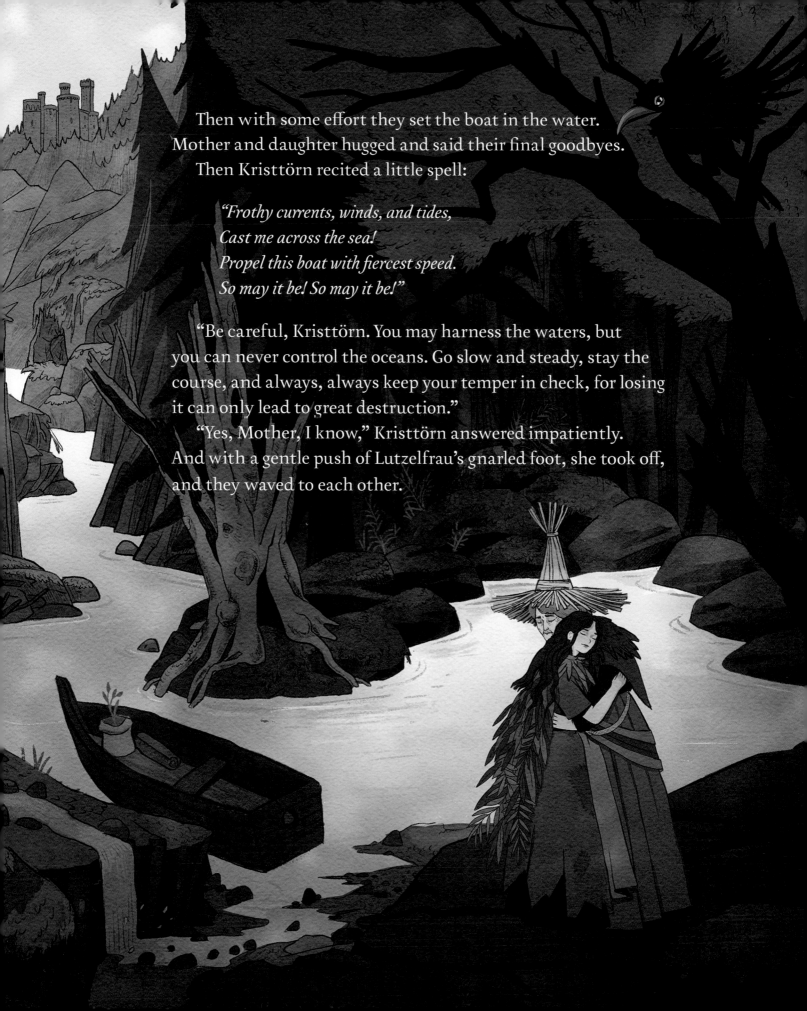

Then with some effort they set the boat in the water.
Mother and daughter hugged and said their final goodbyes.
Then Kristtörn recited a little spell:

"Frothy currents, winds, and tides,
Cast me across the sea!
Propel this boat with fiercest speed.
So may it be! So may it be!"

"Be careful, Kristtörn. You may harness the waters, but
you can never control the oceans. Go slow and steady, stay the
course, and always, always keep your temper in check, for losing
it can only lead to great destruction."

"Yes, Mother, I know," Kristtörn answered impatiently.
And with a gentle push of Lutzelfrau's gnarled foot, she took off,
and they waved to each other.

The small boat floated down the Rhine, winding and twisting along to where it eventually emptied into the enormous, wild North Sea. From there it continued down through the oceans, unimpeded in its journey, fueled by the swiftness spell that Kristtörn had cast. But she was not satisfied.

Faster! Faster! Faster! Kristtörn used the full extent of her powers, but still she wasn't satisfied with the boat's momentum. Faster still and the boat began to creak. She dropped her hand into the water, churning the waves, until she had created a raging maelstrom. The boat rocked and creaked so violently that the sides splintered off, until it was nothing more than a raft. Kristtörn clung to the edges, trying desperately to stop the storm with her powers as the wind whipped around her and the waves crashed over her.

Finally, the winds died down. Drenched with seawater, and exhausted from the storm, she laid down and slept.

What remained of her boat now drifted aimlessly for thousands of miles into the endless sea. A family of leopard seals emerged from the water and helped guide the vessel to a large mass of land in the distance.

Eventually, her raft ran aground on a shore of solid ice.

Wearily, the young girl looked out of the boat at the vast emptiness of the frozen, windswept ice plains and the never-ending gray sky.

At last, at last! I've reached the North Pole! she thought, and then she collapsed back onto the boards and fell into an even deeper sleep.

Little did Kristtörn know that she had actually reached the undiscovered continent of Antarctica—the opposite end of the globe from her brother's North Pole.

By and by, a pair of mismatched red and blue eyes over a large orange beak peered curiously at the wreckage, a yellow-feathered plume cocked to the side. These belonged to a young macaroni penguin named Elsmere.

He gazed for a moment at the beautiful girl sleeping soundly but nearly frozen under a wet woolen blanket as she clutched the small holly tree. He called out to his brothers and sisters, who were fishing for cod in a nearby cove:

"Slippery snowcaps, come and see what I've found! I think it may be a human!"

But the other penguins, already annoyed that he wasn't helping them fish, dismissed him.

"Not again, Elsmere! Stop being silly. There's never been a human down here before."

"It's probably just a bunch of tangled sea kelp. Can't you see we're busy? We need to finish before the sun goes down!"

But he persisted. "No, it's a human girl, and she looks frozen. We must help her."

Finally, out of curiosity, they ran and joined him. When they saw he was right—it was indeed a human, and she would never survive the night as she was—they pulled Kristtörn's raft miles and miles across the dark tundra, under the light of the Full Moon, until they reached their home at the foot of the Transantarctic Mountains.

While she slept in his nest of grass and stones, Elsmere cuddled up beside her to keep her warm, occasionally nudging her gently with his beak to see if she would wake. After many hours, she finally blinked her eyes open and looked wide-eyed at her icy surroundings.

"I made it!" she screamed in joy. The other penguins gathered around, surprised to see her awake.

Kristtörn was relieved to see her holly tree had survived the trip. She hugged Elsmere and exclaimed, "I must be very far north! You see, I am on a journey to find my brother. He must be around here somewhere! Have you seen a young boy who looks just like me—with hair just as red and eyes just as green?"

Hearing this, the other penguins burst out laughing. Elsmere shook his feathers at them and then turned to her. "I'm sorry to say, but . . . you are far, far from the North. This is the South Pole!"

Kristtörn's heart sank and her temper flared. Angrily, she began to kick the stones out of the nest as the other penguins scurried away.

All except for Elsmere. "Whoa!" He laughed. "Don't worry, you can stay here with us as long as you need. My nest is your nest!"

Days turned into weeks. And as time passed, Kristtörn grew accustomed to the frigid existence at the end of the earth . . .

She built a hut made of solid ice. In the center she dug a hole in the snow and planted her holly tree, infusing it with her magic to make it take root. "When this tree grows large enough, I will use its branches to make a new boat and sail home."

Elsmere stitched a beautiful white woolen robe for her to keep warm. She wore this always as well as donning her mother's cape of leaves. Her hair grew wild and dark, fiery red, and she adorned it with sprigs of holly and mistletoe.

Because it was always bitter cold in the tundra and winter lasted most of the year in the South Pole, Kristtörn declared that it should always be Yuletide, her favorite season. She taught the penguins all of the traditions and rituals she learned from Mother Lutzelfrau.

One evening, after yet another Yuletide celebration,
a large black bird swooped down out of the blazing white
sky, crash-landing into a snowbank.

The penguins huddled up, ready to defend themselves
against this mysterious intruder. But as Kristtörn approached the snowbank, she realized quickly that it
was old Malachi, whom she had last seen in the ocean
storm so long ago.

He lifted his distinguished beak, faded gray from years
flown by. "My child! I've searched every corner of the earth
for you, and finally, here you are. Could you have picked a more
impossible place to land?!"

"Oh, Malachi, I've missed you!" she cried.

"I bring much news to you from the Old World," the raven said as she knelt down and kissed his head. "But first I must dry the snow from my feathers by the fire."

Kristtörn and Elsmere helped him inside her hut and he shook his feathers dry. Later, they sipped pine needle tea by the fire.

"Your Mother Lutzelfrau, I'm sorry to say, is no more. She has been gone now for some time"—and here he paused with a slight cough as Kristtörn's eyes filled with tears. "But I have news about your brother!"

"My brother!" Kristtörn exclaimed, her grief now quickly turning to joy.

"Yes, your brother, Kristoffer, now goes by the name of Kringle and has built a home in the North Pole. He is now known to the world for his kindness and generosity. Every year, just after the first day of winter, on the eve of a holiday called Christmas, he travels the globe in his sleigh. This sleigh is pulled by a team of reindeer from village to village, bringing gifts to children and spreading joy to all whom he meets. In some parts he is so beloved they have begun to call him St. Nicholas or Sinterklaas."

"Have you seen him? Has he asked about me?"

"I have not seen him, and almost no one has. He moves swiftly while he works and then disappears before anyone can catch him!"

"I will catch him, for no one knows and understands him better than I."

With a new determined energy, she called her council
of penguins together to announce her new plan.

"The time has come. The tree is ready. We will build a new
boat, even stronger than the first, and set sail before this
Christmas Eve!"

They nodded their beaks in agreement, eager to help. She
selected the six bravest and best swimmers of the group to travel
with her.

Elsmere raised his wing. "Can I come, too? I know I'm not a
great swimmer, but I promise to make a jolly companion!"

Kristtörn petted his head. "Of course, silly. I can't wait for
you to meet my brother!"

Kristtörn and her penguin friends finished assembling the boat, just as the Cold Moon was rising in the sky. Then they headed for the coast with Malachi perched at the bow.

They traveled for three days straight, and on Christmas Eve reached the European continent. Kristtörn sailed to all the major port cities one after the other—Lisbon, Venice, Athens, Istanbul, Stockholm, Dubrovnik. She sailed from Marseille to Belfast to St. Petersburg.

At each port, she moored her boat, hidden in the dark of night. Leaving Elsmere to keep watch, and with Malachi perched on her shoulder, she climbed silently onto the wooden docks, leaving a trail of saltwater and seaweed behind her.

She crept quietly along the cobblestone streets, peering through the windowpanes of darkened houses as children slept, looking desperately for her brother.

Malachi warned her not to disturb the sleeping families. But Kristtörn, always impatient, would sometimes stick her head right through their windows and whistle a nightingale song in the hopes that Kristoffer would hear.

She searched for miles among the country farms, where even the animals rustled in their barn stalls at her passing. She sometimes found fresh reindeer tracks in the mud of a barn-yard or a snowbank next to a chimney, and would press on, feeling certain her brother was close at hand.

As the Christmas dawn was breaking, and her search was coming to an end, she happened upon a barn owl named Ruth who was awake and sitting in quiet thought high up in the rafters.

Quickly, she explained her quest.

"What a pity, you've just missed him!" Ruth said.

"You saw him, then?"

"No. But I heard the tinkling of his sleigh bells," said the owl, who was known for her keen hearing. "I flew to the window just in time to see the back of a sled disappear into the night."

With a sigh, Kristtörn headed back to her boat as the sun rose on the horizon. She was too late and would have to try again next year . . .

And so she did. Every Yuletide season she would search again, determined to catch him once and for all.

She tried leaving little gifts of her own at their doorsteps, hoping to catch her brother's eye, but the adults took these gifts— a woven grass doll, a wreath of penguin feathers, or a simple bouquet of holly leaves—to be evil pagan objects. Sometimes a curious child would beg to keep the trinkets, but they were quickly burned in fireplaces, never to be spoken of again.

Each house that she visited was dreaming of the coming
Christmas morning; but, occasionally, some sleepless child would
catch an eerie glimpse of Kristtörn at the window. Some would stir
awake, frightened by the sound of her strange song, only to catch
her disappearing into the night. And it was then that the whispers
about the Christmas Witch began.

As time passed, and more and more caught glimpses of her, the tales of the Christmas Witch spread. Unbeknownst to Kristtörn, children far and wide now eagerly looked for her as expectantly as for Santa Claus—much to their parents' horror.

Finally, after years of searching, Kristtörn, weary and ready to give up for good, found herself in the piazza of the small Italian village of Lucca. The square was deserted, dark and silent with a heavy snow falling and filling the air. Across the square, she spotted a large burly man loading a sack into a sleigh.

"How strange," she whispered to Malachi, "that this man would be traveling like me in the middle of the night, when the rest of the world is asleep." His clothes, too, were completely foreign to this country.

Just then, the moon came out of the clouds and lit up the square, and the man turned and saw her. Right away she recognized him—her brother. Though it had been many, many years, his face was familiar to her. The same red hair, now streaked with gray, and the same emerald eyes that matched her own and twinkled in the moonlight.

A long look of recognition and understanding passed between them. Then Kristtörn pursed her lips and let out the familiar melodic whistle.

She waited in suspense as the snow continued to fall, so long that she thought perhaps the man had gone.

Then through the crisp air came the answering whistle from her brother. Her heart was overjoyed!

But as Kristtörn moved closer to speak to him, she heard the cries of many voices behind her.

"This way! I hear that witch's song coming from the square!"

A mob of men and women descended on the square from all the surrounding streets, holding torches and calling for the Christmas Witch. They were determined this year to be rid of her, once and for all.

"My dear sister," Kristoffer yelled, "you must run away. It is not safe for you here! Run! I shall find you as soon as I can!"

And in a flash, Kris Kringle, with a familiar wink of his eye and a twist of his head, hopped in his sleigh and was carried off into the night air.

Kristtörn ran down the nearest alley with Malachi flying close behind. The mob advanced on her, but she moved like the wind and was faster than they were. Malachi turned around and flapped his wings in their faces to distract them.

"Beware the cursed pet of the Christmas Witch!" they howled as they covered their heads. "She leaves evil objects at our own doors to lure children into the night! She wants to ruin Christmas!"

"Please!" she cried. "I am no enemy of Christmas! I am not evil, I swear it!"

But they ignored her pleas and continued after her.

She ran to the dock, calling to Elsmere, and hopped in her boat. The villagers screamed and yelled at her from the pier, but they were unable to catch her. She and her penguins sailed down the Serchio river, and eventually off into the dark sea.

She returned to her icy fortress, all the while searching for her brother among the clouds in the sky. She was sure he'd never find her once she returned to the South Pole.

Elsmere and the other penguins gathered in a circle around her, and presented her with a Yule log in hopes to cheer her up. As they huddled around the fire, Kristtörn wept. Another year's journey wasted. And now not only had she lost her brother again, but it seemed as if the whole world had turned against her . . .

Suddenly, the sound of distant bells and a streak of light flashed across the sky. They all looked up and witnessed an incredible sight: eight flying reindeer pulling a massive sleigh, with Kristoffer at the helm!

Kristtörn wiped her tears away and jumped up and down. "My brother!"

Kristoffer landed the sleigh with a gentle thud.

Kristoffer and Kristtörn, together at last, sat by the fire. He offered her some gingerbread cookies from his bag while they told each other stories of growing up in worlds so far apart.

"It is good that you have made your home here, Kristtörn. The New World is not safe for you. As for me, I have responsibilities now . . . I have become an important figure in their new Christmas Eve tradition and I must fulfill this destiny."

"Can't I come with you, brother? I can help you deliver your gifts. My penguin friends are surely up for the task!"

Kristoffer held her hand and looked deep into her hopeful eyes.

"No, Kristtörn. You are too different for them to accept. There is no place for you out there. Stay here where you are safe. Someday, I am certain, things will change."

And while Kristtörn contemplated his words, he leapt up with another wink of his eye and a twist of his head, hopped in his sleigh, and disappeared once more.

Now, as you may remember, Kristtörn was prone to losing her temper. As she stared at the burning Yule log, the flames of the roaring fire reflecting in her eyes, she seethed with an increasing rage.

"How is there no place for me out in the world? How could he have chosen them over me?!"

Elsmere hesitantly approached her and quietly asked, "Will you go after him?"

She turned to him. Something was different about her gaze.

"No! I don't need my brother. Lutzelfrau was wrong.
He was never my destiny. All those years searching in vain,
and only to watch my precious Yuletide be destroyed by greed!
My destiny is clear now. I am going to ruin this Christmas
holiday once and for all!"

Kristtörn's anger flowed out of her and the ground began to tremble. Malachi flew around her in a circle, trying to calm her.

"You must not get excited, my child! No need to do anything drastic, now!"

But in her fury, she stomped her feet on the ground three times. The last stomp proved to be the strongest, for it cracked the solid ice floor wide open, swallowing up Kristtörn, Elsmere, and all her penguin companions.

They immediately froze beneath the surface into blocks of solid ice. Not dead—just asleep. And that is where they've remained ever since . . .

As centuries passed, talk of the Christmas Witch was forbidden by parents all over the world. Meanwhile, Kristtörn's ice palace gradually fell into disrepair and slowly disappeared into the icy Antarctic blizzards. Eventually brave explorers from other continents began taking expeditions down there, planting their nations' flags and claiming the South Pole for their own, unaware of its queen, who lay asleep feet beneath the ice.

But slowly the earth warmed, and the movements of the seas changed, and the once-solid glaciers began to melt. And every year, the Christmas Witch's tomb of ice *drip-drip-drips* away . . .

 EPILOGUE

And so now you know that the Christmas Witch was not always evil. In fact, she was my friend.

I watched her grow up in the forest as a kind and caring child, and I watched the world slowly turn against her.

I was there that day when she made that fateful third stomp, and as I flapped my wings and flew away, I watched the ice break open and an avalanche of snow wash over it, sealing her fate.

Let this be a warning that soon she will be back in the world. And she will seek out her destiny to save Christmas . . . or destroy it. Her emerald eyes will open in the blinding light of the early-morning sun, but her heart will still be frozen by the injustice that she suffered. I do not know if she has forever been changed, or if the goodness in her will eventually win out. I only hope I live to see it.

—*Malachi*

END